The Rumble Seat Pony

By C. W. ANDERSON

The Rumble Seat Pony

C.W. Anderson

Macmillan Publishing Co., Inc.
New York
Collier Macmillan Publishers
London

Macmillan Publishing Co., Inc.
866 Third Avenue, New York, N.Y. 10022

Collier Macmillan Canada, Ltd.

Library of Congress catalog card number: 71–127466

ISBN 0-02-705490-X

Printed in the United States of America

10 9 8 7 6 5 4 3

To Melissa, Pam, Peter
and their pony, Vicky

Melissa, Pam and Peter lived in the country. Their grandfather had given the family a little yellow car that he had bought long before when he was young. The children loved it because it had a rumble seat. It was the only car they wanted to ride in. They liked to go exploring over the country roads with their mother.

6

One day, on a back road, they saw a pony in a field near a vacant house. A sign on a tree in the field said, "House for Sale & Pony Cheap."

8

They saw that the pony was very dirty and
looked sad and lonesome.

"The poor little thing," said their mother.
"Nobody has taken any care of him for a long
time. He's still got his winter coat and it's all
full of mud and burrs. You children wait here.
I'm going to find out who he belongs to and
why he is being treated like this."

The children went over to the wall and called to the pony. He came to them and seemed glad to see them. The girls did not pet him, because he was so very dirty, but Peter did.

"He has a nice eye," he said. "Maybe if he was clean, he would be nice all over."

Peter had always wanted a pony and a dirty pony was better than no pony.

12

When their mother came back she said,
"The people who lived here tried to sell the
pony and couldn't, so they just left him and
said anyone could have him for whatever they
would pay. So I bought him. We'll take him
home and clean him up. Maybe we can find
a home for him."

"No," said Peter. "Please let's keep him."

They led the pony out of the field. He seemed glad to leave that lonesome place. The children climbed into the rumble seat and they started off. Melissa held the pony's rope while Pam and Peter talked to him. Their mother drove slowly so that the pony could keep up easily.

When they got home, their mother told them to put the pony in the woodshed for the night. "Just feed and water him and let him rest. We'll start to clean him up tomorrow."

Pam gathered an armful of sweet clover while Peter and Melissa fed the pony. He was very hungry.

18

After supper the children took a big basket
and went to gather grass to make a soft bed
for the pony. Soon they had enough and the
pony lay down. Then they said good night
and closed the door.

Early the next morning the children started to work. Their mother had borrowed brushes and a currycomb from neighbors who had horses. They were all eager to know what color the pony really was. As they scrubbed they saw that he was brown and white. More and more loose, matted hair came off as they brushed.

At noon their mother and father came out
to see what they had done.

"He looks so different now," said their
mother. "He's really not a bad-looking pony."

"He's beautiful," said Peter.

24

At last they had combed out all the burrs
and most of the loose hair and washed him
until he shone.

"He really looks nice now," said Melissa.
"It's almost like finding buried treasure,
isn't it?"

"Yes, it is," said Pam. "Let's call him
Treasure."

"Yes, Treasure," said Peter. "I like that."

"Would you like a ride, Peter?" asked Melissa. "I'll lead him."

"Yes," said Peter. First he went up and patted the pony on the nose. "Be good, Treasure," he said. Then Melissa helped him mount. The pony walked quietly as Melissa led him around the lawn. Peter was proud and very happy.

28

Peter got out of school earlier than Pam and Melissa, so he always went for a ride as soon as he got home. All the children loved Treasure, but Peter loved him most of all. Whenever they came to some nice grass or clover, Peter would let him graze.

One Saturday the children overslept. As
soon as they came downstairs, they hurried
out to feed Treasure.

The woodshed door was open and the pony
was gone!

32

The children were very worried and called their parents. "He must have gotten hungry and pushed the latch open," said their father. "We'll all go and look for him after breakfast." But when they sat down to eat Peter was not there.

34

They started calling and looking everywhere, but Peter could not be found. At last they saw him coming down the road leading Treasure.

"Where did you find him?" they asked.

"I knew where he'd go if he was hungry," said Peter. "I just went where the grass was greenest and there he was."

36

One day when they were out riding, a neighbor stopped them and said to their mother, "The committee for Old Home Day would like you and the children to lead the parade with the yellow car and the pony."

"Oh, that will be fun," said their mother. "Won't it?" she asked the children. They were all excited about it. Even Treasure seemed to nod his head.

For days before the parade the children brushed Treasure and combed his mane and tail until they were soft and silky. His coat shone and he looked very handsome.

Peter patted his nose softly. "You are the most beautiful pony in the world," he said.

40

It seemed to the children that the day for the parade would never come, but finally it did. It was a beautiful day.

Down Main Street went the little yellow car and behind it, with Peter riding, came Treasure. After them marched many children with flags and then the band. Everybody clapped and cheered for Treasure, who trotted proudly behind the little yellow car. Melissa and Pam were very happy and Peter was the happiest of all.

A few days later the neighbor who had
asked them to lead the parade came over with
a large box. "For your pony," she said.
"From all the folks around here."

Melissa opened the box and saw a beautiful
red blanket. On it, in gold letters, was the
name "Treasure."

"That will keep him warm at night when
the weather gets cold," said the neighbor.

44

The children tried the red blanket on
Treasure and it fitted perfectly.

"Doesn't he look nice?" said Pam.

"He's beautiful!" said Peter.

46

A NOTE ABOUT THE ILLUSTRATIONS

The drawings for *The Rumble Seat Pony* were done with black Prismacolor crayon on smooth illustration board, in order to approximate as closely as possible the effect of lithograph crayon on stone, my favorite black-and-white medium. As lithographs must be done to the exact size of the finished illustrations, they are not satisfactory for a small-sized book where the details of faces must be shown. But since the Prismacolor crayon does not smudge, it can be handled on board in the same way as lithograph crayon on stone and will produce a similar effect.

C. W. Anderson